Published by
North Atlantic Books
Berkeley, California

Cover art by Ruby Roth
Book design by Ruby Roth
Printed in China

Bad Day is sponsored and published by the Society for the Study of Native Arts and Sciences (dba North Atlantic Books), an educational nonprofit based in Berkeley, California, that collaborates with partners to develop cross-cultural perspectives, nurture holistic views of art, science, the humanities, and healing, and seed personal and global transformation by publishing work on the relationship of body, spirit, and nature.

North Atlantic Books' publications are available through most bookstores. For further information, visit our website at www.northatlanticbooks.com or call 800-733-3000.

NOTE: Paper bags are great to play with, but *plastic bags* are bad for the environment and no good for fun. Never put a plastic bag over your head.

Library of Congress Cataloging-in-Publication data is available from the publisher upon request.

Printed and bound by Qualibre (NJ)/PrintPlus, March 2019, in Hong Kong, Job #190366

1 2 3 4 5 6 7 8 9 Qualibre/PrintPlus 24 23 22 21 20 19

North Atlantic Books is committed to the protection of our environment. We partner with FSC-certified printers using soy-based inks and print on recycled paper whenever possible.

Other books by Ruby Roth:

That's Why We Don't Eat Animals, *Vegan Is Love*, *V Is for Vegan*, *The Help Yourself Cookbook for Kids*

Bad Day

Written and Illustrated
by Ruby Roth

North Atlantic Books
Berkeley, California

It does not matter what other people do;

what matters is the kind of person you want to become.

—Rabbi Mordecai Finley, PhD

Don't ask me, 'cause

I DON'T KNOW WHY!

Some peace and
some quiet, please!
Finally, yesss.

No noise and no people who'll try
to make me feel better—
they make my face redder!
At last, I can finally...

Sighhh!!!...

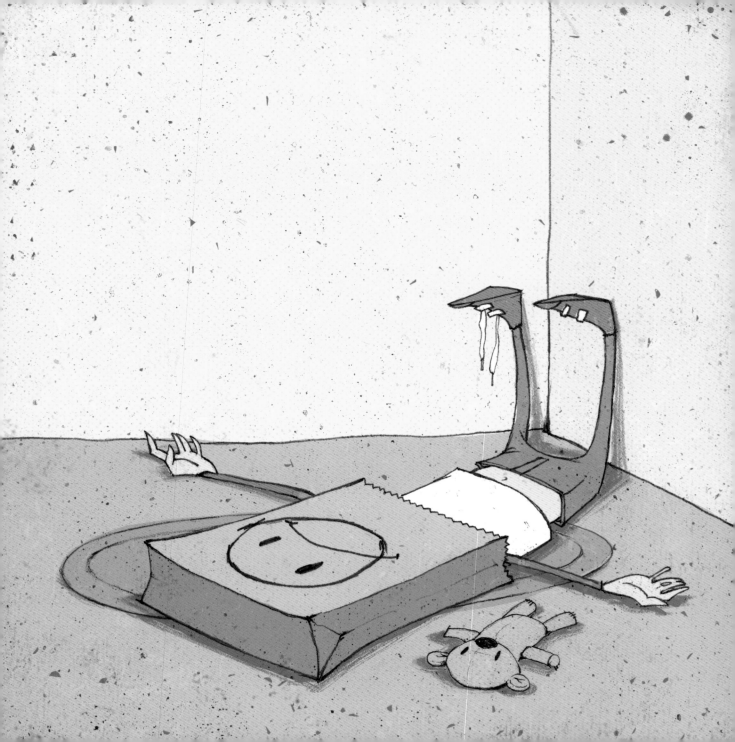

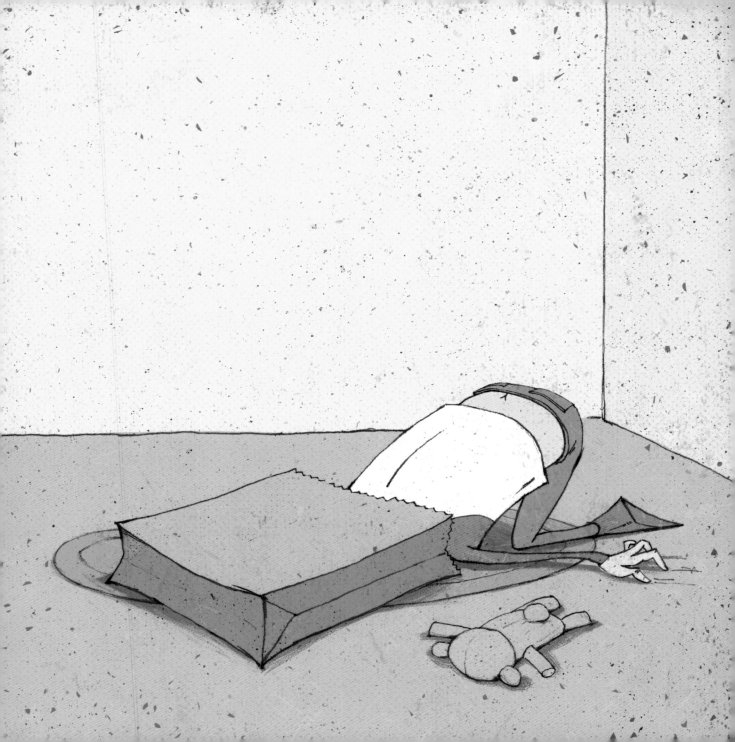

I did NOT like today.
It can **SHOO!** Go away.
It couldn't be over too soon.

Hmmm...

Wait a minute...
I'll say...

I'll be okay,
no matter the day,
no matter what goes on outside.
No matter the people,
their words or their ways,
I am my own feelings guide.

Hey...

It's some kind of magic,
this space deep inside.
I can quietly hide and decide
which feelings to feel and
which are most real,
I wouldn't have known 'til I tried.

Now I'm more clear!
Hey! It's quite fun in here—
just me and my feelings and thoughts.

I can always return
and find something to learn.
My body's the best thinking spot.

Well...

It's not been a year,
but I will reappear.
I can live in the world
with more cheer.

'Cause even a BAD day
can teach you some good,
and that feelings are
nothing to fear.

About North Atlantic Books

North Atlantic Books (NAB) is an independent, nonprofit publisher committed to a bold exploration of the relationships between mind, body, spirit, and nature. Founded in 1974, NAB aims to nurture a holistic view of the arts, sciences, humanities, and healing. To make a donation or to learn more about our books, authors, events, and newsletter, please visit www.northatlanticbooks.com.

North Atlantic Books is the publishing arm of the Society for the Study of Native Arts and Sciences, a 501(c)(3) nonprofit educational organization that promotes cross-cultural perspectives linking scientific, social, and artistic fields. To learn how you can support us, please visit our website.